BIGFOOT

BIGFOOT

A Tale Told Twice

jo nambiar

PARTRIDGE

ISBN: Hardcover   978-1-4828-7496-9
             Softcover   978-1-4828-7495-2
             eBook   978-1-4828-7494-5

Print information available on the last page.

To order additional copies of this book, contact
Partridge India
000 800 10062 62
orders.india@partridgepublishing.com

www.partridgepublishing.com/india

Introduction

As stories go, dear Reader, this one is a dawdler;
For neither is it a romance, horror nor a thriller.
I have thrown caution to the wind in my alacrity,
To tell a tale in rhyme, and have taken the liberty
To even dismiss poetic meter, hoping the essentials,
That the story demands of my writing credentials,
Will help you too find rhythm and make good sense
Of my quaint story and my brash poetic license.

PART - 1

1

Sneha was a student of biodiversity
At the North Eastern Hill University.
I, on the other hand, had business planned,
And some dusty farmland inherited from Granddad.
Okay, let's just say, I was actually unemployed,
But with plans afoot and funds deployed.
Or maybe it was the other way around?
For, by year two thousand and ten, I had run aground!

2

"You need to focus on just one thing, Jo.
One thing at a time and your money will grow."
Such bum advice you receive on an average
Every week, turning your best plans to carnage.
You nod or "*ahan*!" and to listen you pretend,
But sooner or later they reach out to your girlfriend
With "there are many healthier men out there,
With much better inheritance, career and flair!"

3

A cute girl, this Sneha, I christened her "Snaps",
It suited her spirit and her Nepali temper perhaps.
I've done everything to keep her scant attention,
But a new boy-scout always appears on the horizon.
She pays flirty attention to one Rahul and one Ashish,
So she could walk me on a transparent leash.
On tenterhooks, self-doubt and bated breath,
We still die in many ways before our deaths!

4

Then there was poor Gita Singh, my sole admirer,
Always tugging, making me look like a philanderer.
Stylish Gita, a woman very wholesomely urban,
Whose wardrobe was nothing less than mink and ermine.
If you think you have clothes that are designer,
She'll sashay past you wrapped in a Pashmina.
I stupidly complimented Gita for her long hair!
Sneha's mood since then nearly drove me to despair!

5

When Gita pinched my cheek and called me cute,
I should have known why Sneha remained so mute.
It must have worked like Sodium Chloride to injury,
Sneha's smile didn't betray her intense fury.
I concluded all was fine. I wasn't keen on Gita,
Sneha was my girl, not that urban senorita.
But now convincing Sneha about that was another story.
You could end up feeling culpable, in pain and gory.

6

Damned between a "conquest" and a lady friend,
Sneha's aloofness taunted my male ego no end.
Ask any man. The unattainable always beckons you
Like an adventure. Requiring guile before the coup.
In comparison, Gita was discernable, lacked mystery,
Her mink and Pashmina albeit stylish artistry.
But Sneha, despite her wispy, straight, hill-folk hair
Still commanded awe as if challenging you to dare.

7

To give just the backdrop of my story, dear reader:
Sneha, Gita, Ashish, Rahul. Myself no bystander.
I hated Ashish and Rahul as she did Pashmina and mink
Sneha also hated Gita – called her an "artificial thing."
The rest of the University blissfully adapted,
Ignorant of the pangs and drama being enacted
Each day in the region of our heart and mind.
I so needed some space, a place where I could unwind!

8

So before we turned ourselves into mental wrecks,
I began planning a get-away, a holiday, a trek!
A trek! Appealing and inexpensive as it sounds,
Always took you to places well out of bounds
Of university traffic, wannabes and rich bachelors,
Away from the competition and detractors.
Today, I wonder how that idea got itself planted
In my head. Suddenly, all other plans I recanted.

9

Sneha held bio-diversity very close to her heart,
But that's OK. For me, her attention was set apart.
Petite, short-haired, such wispy hair you'll never see,
She exuded intellect, and regarded lethargy an allergy.
She wasn't descended from any famed line of scholars,
But placed among her peers, she was cerebrally taller.
To hold her attention for months I had to play tricks,
Now the idea of a holiday really gave her the kicks.

10

Knowing Sneha was stressed and under pressure,
I said, "Snaps, let's get away somewhere together."
My announcement must have hit her like a jackpot,
Then again I knew exactly what she must have thought.
"Seychelles or Bali?" she immediately queried.
"Oh, just a trek around Nepal," (I had readied)
"You know, wilderness, camping and all that,
The kind of holiday that don't make you fat?"

11

"But Jo, what's really in it for both of us?"
My sweet Sneha now began to create a fuss.
"Snaps, you're a keen student of biodiversity.
Come we'll make it a study and some festivity."
"No, Jo. Lounging in casinos is what I won't do;
And besides, I'm quite tired of your Katmandu.
I want to sunbathe, shop, and taste good food,
And be seen at nightclubs with an eligible dude!"

12

A week or two of more dogged convincing,
Left Sneha with no more words for mincing.
"Okay, Nepal it is, but if you'll schedule
A trek-plan to prove the existence of Beyul."
I blinked. "Beyul? What, do you mean by that?
It's a Buddhist yarn, a tall story, hardly a fact.
You're chasing some lama's shaggy-dog yarn,"
I couldn't resist the gibe and the sham yawn.

13

While she ranted on in complaining oratory,
I wondered where she got ideas so exploratory.
Whatever happened to Seychelles and Bali?
I intended a cheap trek but not reckless folly!
Sneha emphasized, "We're not running from people.
We are on a trek to prove we're a great couple.
When we return we'll be a picture of success,
With our pics on page 3, in my little black dress."

14

And like a persistent upstaged schoolgirl,
Sneha spent hours on phone and on Google.
Till she came up with a high density image
Of a thousand square miles with just one village.
Pointing at a grey spot in the snow laden collage,
She swore she saw Beyul's forest and foliage.
I cried, "There are no more secret valleys, Snaps!
We're living in the world of satellite maps!"

15

Take "*Shangri La*" in Lost Horizon, a book by James Hilton
Is nothing but an imaginary valley, a 1933 fiction.
"*El Dorado*" was not even that, an old wife's tale at best.
A city of gold in America, an ancient mariner's quest.
Secret valley, forbidden valley, hidden valley and *Jannath*,
Even the *Lost Valley* of Turok was hardly on our trek path.
Now this Beyul, like *Jataka*, was another Buddhist fiction,
To humour Sneha need I agree to such a destination?

16

"I've found Beyul! Beyul!" when she jumped up in glee,
I seriously began to calculate the Sherpa guide's fee.
"Don't look so vexed and worried, my dear Jo,
We'll just await the summer melt of the snow.
Beyul's secret pass opens for only three weeks.
We'll start out trek when the summer heat peaks.
Into the secret valley we'll sneak in and out,
Before the snow returns and shuts up the mouth."

17

To cut a long story short, I agreed feebly with her,
We went about shopping for snow jackets and fur.
At least my enthusiasm shown made her happyish,
She now paid less attention to Rahul and Ashish.
She dropped all odd work and part time venture
To engage more fruitfully in our secret adventure.
She stopped participating in debates and student politics
At which she was a live-wire with famed invectives.

18

We held a press-meet to announce our departure.
Sneha vivaciously described Behul's greener pastures.
The Times of India reporter tried to believe in our hunch
Of Beyul existence, provided we served lunch.
Otherwise his report might be relegated to the inane.
He could publish it, but he didn't want to sound insane.
Finally nothing was reported, despite the comestible bribe.
You should have heard Sneha's fury and Nepali diatribe!

19

Three months later we were up in Nepal's foothills,
Camped in fortified ice huts to face the mountain chills.
Acclimatizing thus for a week before we found us a jeep
To traverse the glacial moraines to a Sherpa village heap.
In the frigid Himalayas we finally hired some mules,
And rode for a day before using our climbing tools.
Arriving at a craggy knoll the Sherpas stopped in submission,
Frightened to travel beyond and scared by superstition.

20

Their loud characteristic banter now became whispers,
As if some mountain ghoul had given them the shivers.
They congregated and sighed, undecided what distance to go.
I failed to see a single hazardous sign in all that glorious snow.
Sneha spoke to them, heard their woes and smiled at me in turn;
I didn't care what their excuses were; I smiled at her in return.
We were here for a trek and the mountains we shall roam,
Sans guides or Serpas, we even knew our way back home.

21

Could this be the clincher that we were on the right track?
If Beyul was beyond, now there was no turning back.
It was in the Sherpa blood, very part of their tradition;
Their guides never abandon a mountain expedition,
Unless some evil beyond their comprehension,
Threatened their lives or made off with their ration.
For Sneha, however, it was a triumph of her belief!
For me, well, I still had Sneha, and some needed relief!

22

A Sherpa guide passed me a bottle of some local wine.
The farewell drink warmed me and made me feel divine.
The Sherpa were full of apologies; all I could do was smile.
Sneha hobnobbed with them in Nepalese whispers for a while.
She appeared to comfort them while they kept cautioning her.
I wondered what it was all about, what did we have to fear?
Finally, they left peering furtively at me swigging their wine.
I raised a mocking farewell toast to show I was doing fine.

23

With only maps, compasses and legs to power,
We climbed a whole day to camp at dusk hour.
The following day Sneha and I looked over
A mountain gorge we could barely maneuver.
All that day, to the bottom slowly descending,
Our search for Beyul was nearing its ending.
Beyond this point with our lives we could pay,
For our route and purpose was now only hearsay.

24

One more day's march from that gorge to a ridge,
In whiteout conditions we crossed a footbridge.
Then through the storm we saw on a rocky face,
A long vertical fissure starting up in the haze.
From some invisible point at the top of the rocks,
Dividing the mountain into two massive blocks.
And behold! Before us in the wall-face there lay
The gap to Beyul, the legendary passageway!

25

Our breathing grew labored, our eyes were moist,
Sneha made it mandatory, so a flag we did hoist.
A sign-board was written for others to take note;
Should future adventurers at some point promote
Our fabled valley to tourists. So let it be known
That "Snaps and Jo had to the world first shown,
The only mountain-pass to the region of Beyul."
We thought that sign-board looked really cool.

26

The frozen mountain-side was suddenly warm,
With sweltering hot air like my Granddad's farm.
Humid gas blew rowdily out of the Himalayan pass,
Like a giant expelling wind while we stood at its arse.
The wind caused to sweat every hair and follicle,
Indicating the region inside was torrid and tropical.
Beyul's climate was believed to have such docility;
And also to be the home of the abominable Yeti!

27

Yeti, Abominable Snowman, Sasquatch or Great Ape,
Allegedly creatures like us both in stride and in shape.
But colossal, more than eight, perhaps ten feet tall,
A large head with each eye-socket like a tennis ball.
Obnoxious and dangerous if encountered they say,
I think this silly legend of the Yeti is here to stay.
Dumb primate that apparently survived the ice age.
But for Sneha, really, I wouldn't give this half a page.

28

Now the pass, our passage, this gap in the rock
Was a march of just seven hours by the clock.
Not knowing that, and since the hour was late,
At the mouth of the pass we camped and stayed.
Till dawn, to tackle the pass in full daylight.
A foray into even the entrance was scary at night.
Of our journey now all that was really left
Was to march through this narrow mountain cleft.

29

The allure of Beyul's pass disrupted our sleep.
Though pooped, at night at the pass I would peep.
The furtive balmy air so beckoned to and fro,
That before dawn we were up and rearing to go.
A sumptuous breakfast and coffee piping hot,
Revitalized our bodies, motivated our thought.
We now packed with renewed vigor and energy,
Our keen anticipation turned now into frenzy!

30

The first few meters of the pass was very eerie.
Five feet wide, flowing water, Sneha had a theory:
That "a fault in the earth's crust formed a small crack,
And it widened by erosion every time it snowed back.
Soft rock gave way to flowing water, wind and rain,
Creating a channel, this pass, for the valley to drain."
"A cool theory, Snaps, but you know what's weird,
I think it's something about me that our Sherpas feared."

31

The pass we navigated was a winding crevice
With no trace of snowflakes, hail or melting ice.
Instead vines and lichen were copiously growing,
Interlacing, intertwining, trailing and overhanging.
Sheer walls rise a thousand meters on either side,
Sometimes narrowing the path till walls nearly collide.
From barely two feet it sometimes widened to thirty
Where small tropical life forms were evident in plenty.

32

A clamor of noises started where it was wide
Hissing, squeals, hoots and threats implied.
Sometimes when our feet splashed in a creek
It started twitters, chirps, clicks and even shrieks
Of insect, cicada, fly, beetle and maybe an owl,
But oddly, no sounds of any larger animal on the prowl.
Camera in hand, Sneha clicked everything she eyed.
Thus four hours went by. We were only half a km inside!

33

"Jo, its only midday now," Sneha felt in charge!
"There's no danger; no flippant Yeti's at large.
This hour until midday is the brightest in this gap,
Marching another three hours and going by my map,
We'll reach the Beyul valley, and just in case we don't,
Why not camp tonight? Our discovery we'll postpone."
"Snaps, the sooner we reach Beyul, the sooner we get out.
Snowfall here is sudden, and completely shuts the mouth."

34

Indeed a sobering thought, Sneha fell quite silent.
No radio or mobile phones and snowstorms so violent.
Satellite couldn't pierce this fog, this haze and precipitation.
The pass is unseen by helicopter, jet or expedition.
But cheer, there's no instant threat of falling ice or snow.
Surely, it must only be the end of the meltdown now.
For water trickled everywhere and sometimes it gushed,
The three weeks window we could use if we only rushed.

35

Midday came like a bolt, a shock in every way
When we received the elusive sun's every ray.
Passing overhead shining straight into the crevice,
Startling everyone, from the wood owl to the mice.
Reflecting light off wet, sparkling glacial debris,
Dew-drops on creepers like a bizarre Christmas tree.
Like an alien ship suddenly catching us in its dragnet,
Powerful blinding death rays on an unsuspecting planet.

36

Hardly recovered from the bright death ray
An amazing darkness fell just after midday.
The sun reached the other shoulder of the cleft
Plunging our pass once again into its familiar depth
Of darkness with footpaths very deceitful,
Slowing the progress of our trek to Beyul.
We labored on seemingly forever in the pass,
By evening we neared an open field of grass.

37

Behold Beyul! We grabbed each other in joy.
"Kudos Sneha!" Though this trek was indeed my ploy.
The pass behind us, again just a gap in the wall,
Before us was a mild, calm and most of all
A valley that belonged just to Sneha and me.
(At least until weeks later, when she reports to page 3)
Dusk was upon us, time to quickly find a campsite
And secure the spot against any threat in the night.

38

We walked over the grass keeping close to the cliff,
I looked for a nook or a cave on the mountain relief.
Another hour of marching filled us with exhilaration,
Fresh cool air caused us to experience no perspiration.
It was almost twilight; I finally found a site to camp,
It was high ground, an overhanging rock like a ramp.
Some water below reflected a rocky face submerged
Of the mountain through which we had just emerged.

39

I feared whether we'd moved too far from the gap
Of our only escape route if something should hap.
In an hour and a half as darkness filled the Beyul valley,
I gathered sticks, stones and lengths of vines to tally.
Our overhanging rock could pass for a habitable cavern,
To camouflage the entrance I used canvas and fern.
I booby-trapped the stockade, an intruder if he crept
Would be hurt severely before he learnt where we slept.

40

Then a "yelp" in the distance we suddenly heard.
It was cause for alarm. The first time we feared!
The bark was perhaps of some wolf or Great Dane,
We might not after all be on top of the food chain!
So a casual little camp of canvas might not suffice
But like Nepal I couldn't build a site of fortified ice.
Defenses were needed here. If we called for help
Who would find us here? The creature that yelped!

41

So, with no one here that we could befriend,
We built a place we could best defend.
Like Robinson Crusoe's cave and stockade
Into which our precious supplies we laid.
No creature could surprise us from the top
Unless some boulder should accidently drop.
Guarding the camp would have been a trifle
Like Crusoe had I somehow salvaged a rifle.

42

I quickly cut us two cudgels for weapons,
Sneha laughed at my martial art actions
When I demonstrated the attack I planned
Upon intruders whether single or in a band.
"Had I a firearm," I said. Sneha laughed aside.
"Jo, you couldn't hit a barn from the inside!
We're better off unarmed and posing no threat,
To innocent creatures that we haven't even met!"

43

Soon fatigue ensured that we passed out
Without care of our unique whereabout.
We slept like babies both Sneha and I
Undisturbed by mosquito, insect or fly.
I imagined many times that I heard that yelp
In the night. First Sneha did and then myself.
I dreamt again of that midday's death ray,
Bright beam of sunlight in an action replay.

44

Startled next morning, an awareness of light
And a mellow sunny glow, an otherworldly sight.
Steam, mist or dust hazed the mountain horizon.
Was this grassland also home of deer and bison?
The mountain wall abounded the valley on all sides
Like a fortress or cliff face that zealously hides
Thick forests in the distance, trees of massive girth.
If ever there was paradise it must be this on earth.

45

Sneha had a theory: And this really took the cake!
"A volcano's caldera! This valley was once a lake.
The rocky sides eroded. The crater filled like a bowl.
Climate became docile with hot-springs in control.
The mountain pass we took was nothing but a crack,
On the South side of this bowl from eons way back,
Draining water and soil and keeping the valley flat
And venting high temperatures just like a thermostat."

46

Before we could explore the near areas of Beyul
I tried to gather firewood and dry items for fuel.
"Never leave base camp without food or pelt"
Thumb rules of mountaineering in Beyul too I held.
"Can you remember when we'd last eaten, Snaps?
I did eat something some eight hours ago perhaps."
Hunger appears stymied here, even thirst foiled!
We were not starving though our bodies had toiled!

47

Before I continue my narration of this odd event,
For the record I note here our sworn testament.
That we never ate food, solid, liquid or gruel,
For the rest of our stay in the valley of Beyul.
We had backpacked sufficient stocks in can and tin
Of processed food for a month and doses of vitamin.
But we never felt hungry to our awe and amazement.
It wasn't a digestive disorder or a stomach ailment.

48

Sneha could not theorize why we could not ingest,
We carried no drugs if some new virus was to infect.
The puzzle of our stomachs sans pain or appetite
Confounded, but did not spoil our sleep at night.
We tried to taste and bite at food, baked and boiled,
Something in the air at Beyul appears to have foiled,
Thwarted taste buds that made edibles taste like fodder.
We found foodstuff distasteful and repelled by its odour.

49

We experienced no weakness not even a mild dehydration,
Occasionally we drank water but it was lost in perspiration.
Oblivion of hunger gave more time to explore our campsite,
To understand the grassland, the flora and the parasites.
Sporadically a geyser would squirt hot steam into the air,
Momentarily exciting, like gas balloons released at a fair.
Sneha was cheery and excited, her beautiful face a bliss.
Wouldn't Rahul and Ashish give an arm and a leg for this?

50

We explored a bit, straying very little from the fence
Of sticks, the stockade that I'd created for our defense.
The first day in Beyul was spent in consolidating camp,
Finding ways of keeping a fire lit in a hurricane lamp,
With urgency we went about stocking and securing,
Set a hearth of stones, found a spring of water running.
A vine to hang a mirror and for useful niches in the cave
What articles to discard and what bits and pieces to save.

51

The following six days that constituted our first week
We walked great distances with nothing to seek,
But to look upon rambling grasslands in the valley;
Limpid pools and thick forests sitting forebodingly.
It became clear that the valley was uninhabited
But for birds and rodents that we rarely sighted.
Sneha made notes on matters of biodiversity
For submission to the North-Eastern Hill University.

52

For over a week, barely a part of Beyul did we roam,
It was time to return to Nepal and then home.
We didn't want the snow to begin falling back
Into the passage where it would invariably pack
Into an inaccessible heap that would seal the cleft,
Trapping us in this odd valley or all that was left
Of an unfathomable paradise here on this planet.
Call it Beyul, El Dorado, Shangri-La or Jannath!

53

So we repacked our stocks, and food, plate and glass,
Though in ten days we'd not eaten even a blade of grass.
Our sojourn at this valley in our cameras we recorded,
In our hearts the thrill of all that we had discovered
Of an almost windless basin, balmy starless nights;
Rivulets flowing gently shining crystal clear to our sight.
Of mornings of mild sunlight, middays that were cool,
And exotic footage of the mountain passage to Beyul.

54

Now packed and ready to Beyul we bade farewell,
With notices written for future travelers to this dell
Posted at our campsite which we largely left intact,
Located on high ground for anyone else to enact
Our curious drama, when they read it off page three
And view our recordings for which we'd charge a fee,
Or sell our video footages to a TV channel that'll agree
To talk to us like Karan does, over coffee, or was it tea?

55

We were done repacking when we heard a familiar yelp
Carried downwind from miles away, was it a cry for help?
It was an ominous sound, both of us had quite forgotten;
Having found no large wildlife, only traces of small rodent.
Since the week that we had explored portions of this vale.
This yelping now disturbed us and really made Sneha pale.
The crying indicated a creature harassed or prone to harass,
I suggested we march pronto towards our mountain-pass.

56

Sneha had a theory, I requested her to please shut up.
We weren't going to be some mountain creature's sup.
Contingency was upon us, bio-diversity could wait awhile,
Theories never saved human life like two legs to a mile!
We set off at a brisk pace, ears strained to hear the bark,
Marching to reach the mountain pass before it turned dark.
I wish I knew what kind of creature we were running from,
Sneha didn't want to know, her anxiety made her numb.

57

Fear has a strange effect on mankind's body chemistry,
Womankind's more hilarious; their fear is like an injury.
A constant whimpering, looking for someone to blame,
Sneha's fear changed to anger when I tried to proclaim
That the yelp might after all be just an obnoxious fox
Sniffing a trail of our food stock or even her nylon socks.
As we broke into a run the yelping intensified from behind,
I often glanced back, but there was nothing there to find.

58

More trouble awaited us despite this nagging one behind.
We ran, stumbled, lurched and staggered only just to find
That the pass was already flowing and filling up with snow.
Sneha sniveled in despair, "I think we're done for, Jo!"
Ice, hail and slush was falling from the rocky cliff above,
As if the menace behind us was with nature, hand-in-glove
To prevent us from leaving the valley which we had entered
Despite the Sherpa's warning and the prayers we'd tendered.

59

The persistent yelping now made us both spin around.
I picked up a heavy cudgel, swung it and hit the ground.
The creature was approaching; it was just yards away,
If it was a wolf or bear, shouldn't it howl or bay?
Stranded we awaited, something alarming for sure,
Our wildest fancy hadn't primed us to meet a Chihuahua!
A yelping mouse-like creature, it seemed a friendly dog!
Sneha, petrified, was convinced it was a venomous frog.

60

We stood frozen in comic relief and unmitigated fear,
A Chihuahua in front of us and a mountain in the rear.
It sat there before us merrily wagging a noodle for a tail,
Was his yelping that had startled us so often in this dale?
"Hey doggie, come here, what's your God damn name?
If you're a wild dog then how come you act so very tame?
Your breed is not a local one. Snaps, isn't he a Chihuahua?
I thought your pedigree lived in Mexico, or is it in Okinawa?"

61

And as the mountain pass closed the dog gaily wagged away,
As if he had designed and planned the need for us to stay.
Sneha feeling weak in the knees sat down to ease her shock,
I helped unhitched her haversack and sat myself down on a rock.
Our march had been too stressful and utterly disappointing,
Prospects of being trapped for a year was even more frustrating.
The outside world would eventually come to terms with our loss.
Imagine receiving a posthumous Distinguished Trekking Cross!

62

Sneha blamed herself for all this and was inclined to despair,
Circumstances warranted it, her disposition was past repair.
Though it was time to take stock and accept the inevitable,
I tried to explain that the situation was not exactly irrevocable.
I tried to have Sneha understand she was not to blame.
It was something preordained, destiny had played a game.
At least we were in paradise or some Eden unconfirmed.
What if our forgotten hunger and love for food returned!

63

Thank God, we were healthy and not lost a gram of weight
And our stamina was remarkable and sturdy was our gait.
Inexplicably we didn't tire nor did we feel any disease,
Though we hadn't defecated we felt no pressure to release.
We could surely live a year shorn of needs, desires and sickness,
The rat race outside had certainly reduced lives to recklessness.
"Think *holiday*, Snaps! Think *vacation*! A year's sabbatical *free*!
This is a higher state of existence great sages chose voluntarily."

64

Sneha took some time to recover and some more time to imbibe,
The thought of living one whole year sans university or diatribe.
We slowly stood up gazing at Beyul, our home for the year below,
Yelp, the Chihuahua was marching ahead urging us to follow.
We retraced our steps back to the nook, the camp of our creation
To reestablish our base once again and prepare for a long vacation.
Like prisoners back in their cells at dusk, lost in myriad thoughts,
We hardly spoke to each other, just lay in our separate hammocks.

65

I saw Yelp in the dusky darkness wandering among our things.
He sniffed and smelled at everything as if they were all jinxed.
He raised his hind leg against our stuff to mark his territory
But nothing squirted out at our camp so he tried at the periphery.
Poor dog, he too was afflicted by the phenomenon blighting us,
No thirst, no hunger and as a result, not even a piss to pass.
I rolled off the hammock and tried to feed him a biscuit,
He turned his head away as if to say he wouldn't risk it.

66

I was beseeched with questions about the Chihuahua.
We'd hardly known him, not for more than even an hour.
Could Yelp be an indicator that others lived in Beyul valley?
Would he show us the way to them or would he dilly-dally?
How do you keep a dog that won't depend on you for food?
Was Yelp man's best friend just because he was in the mood?
Anyway, how far does a Chihuahua run, like in a single day?
Did Yelp belong to anyone or was he just a stray?

67

One Sunday at dawn, to make further conquests,
I decided to take a tour of Beyul's mighty forests.
Leaving Sneha and Yelp safely at the campsite,
I traversed the broad grasslands to some other side.
To the edge where the woods began very sparsely,
As I walked into the jungle the silence was unearthly.
I noted the direction was up-wind that I had entered,
My odour would not reach anyone before I appeared.

68

The tropical forest would have a botanist confounded.
I recognized most trees and yet it left me astounded.
Beyul was a gene-pool of the world's best wood;
Iron wood, rosewood, rubber wood, sandalwood.
There grew teak-trees, sal, Hollong and Margosa,
Sacred fig, bread fruit, mahogany and Ashoka.
Varieties of mango, Palmyra and horse chestnut,
Why, the place even had banyan, orange and coconut!

69

Fruits fell, decomposed in heaps and mounds.
I came from a world where hunger abounds.
None to pick them, no market, no mouth,
No hunters despite rivers full of trout.
I carried a cudgel with a spike at the end,
But Beyul didn't have predators for me to contend.
No herds, no population, no collective noun,
If two is company, here three could be a small town.

70

What danger lurks where predators are not hungry?
Where there are not enough of you to look at or envy?
A place where you do not encounter a competing force,
Where fresh air just happens to be your main course.
Where it doesn't matter whether you're clothed or in the buff,
Where you don't need to "keep up" or pointlessly bluff.
What pain is there in a place free of disease and starvation?
Wow! Without hunger, the world's such a different equation!

71

No paths existed in the thyme-lined grassy undergrowth,
Paths happen only when creatures go back and forth.
I even paused by a large pool of clear tepid water
Expecting to see living creatures congregate and chatter.
Like we see on Discovery TV and National Geographic.
Suddenly the nature of Beyul felt absolutely horrific.
It was then that a strong odour assailed my nostril,
Rancid smell of a mountain goat, yak or mandrill!

72

The stench blew up-wind growing rank and fetid,
To the direction of the wind this alert I was indebted.
A creature grazing nearby had a distinct body stink,
Should be larger than Yelp and hairier I think.
But before I could even move to duck out of sight,
A large breasted primate appeared on the pool's other side.
Ten-foot-tall, upright, a female ape so gargantuan
She might easily have overtaken King Kong or Hanuman.

73

God, what a stench? Acrid and malodorous,
What a pong? So clammy and disharmonious!
She had sensed me, seen me, even sized me up,
I slinked down frightened like a terrified pup.
Unperturbed she drank water while I feigned around
As if attempting to run, but she stood her ground.
She confidently lifted her colossal head and nostrils,
Sniffing her own shoulder and under her arm-pits.

74

"Oh Jesus!" I exclaimed in morbid fear,
Feeling quite sure that death was near.
"Oh! Oh!" Was all my breath could utter,
While my knees and bowels felt like butter.
I was reduced to shaking, to rapid sweat,
Cringing helplessly from the colossal threat.
"Oh my god", I managed to pray,
"Please let me live just one more day!"

75

She stood still and stared at me to growl
"Grrrrrr!" followed by a high pitched howl.
I froze in terror while she shook her coat,
Running her paw through the hair in her throat.
Then with a sneer that looked like a smile,
She saluted me unexpectedly in military style.
I wondered with which rock I could strike,
Or spear her in the heart with my spike.

76

"Do you like my coat?" A voice articulated.
I looked around but my hopes deflated.
For the friendly voice that I'd just heard
Had emanated from the very creature I feared.
It said, "Your temperament I don't quite admire.
You look even weaker when you perspire.
Look at you, you scrawny little beanpole,
Just keep your violent thoughts in control!"

77

I could never have thought a Yeti could speak
In human tongue, even primitive Nepalese!
But there she stood this monkey's descent
Speaking clear English and no hint of accent.
"Hey what do you think of my furry coat?
Is it better in hue than your Pashmina goat?"
She ruffled, preened then shook and declared
In English for God's sake, I swear by Granddad!

78

"I know your world well, I once lived there,
I've seen and experienced your vanity fair.
Now tell me quick just what you think
Of my tawny coat. Is it better than mink?"
I closed my eyes; was this hallucination?
A mandrill speaking with pith and punctuation!
What could the pressing problem be with her fur?
That she needs my opinion like I was her coiffeur!

79

The reason must be in the thin mountain air.
I would soon wake up. This was a nightmare.
Like in folklore, there was this Rip Van Winkle
Who woke up with a bent back and many a wrinkle.
Delusions happen when you submit to them.
It only requires you to persuasively overwhelm.
I didn't try to arouse, stir myself up or shake;
I could end this nightmare even before I awake.

80

But while it lasted let's just be brave!
No dream has ever landed anyone in a grave.
"Okay monkey girl, just what is it?"
I stood up straight and loudly quipped.
She shook again. She guffawed out loud,
Heaving a chest that was really well endowed.
Then asked with a smirk that resembled a grin,
"Does my coat look like some artificial thing?"

81

"Just what is it you want of me, beast?
Your fur doesn't interest me in the least.
When this dream is done and I awake,
I'll laugh at you till my sides should ache.
But for now let me introduce myself.
I'm Jo Nambiar. What do you call yourself?
Abominable snowman, Yeti, Sasquatch or ape?
And what's with this coat, this smelly drape?"

82

The creature recoiled. She looked very insulted.
And peered into the water where she reflected.
For a moment she fought with her identity crunch;
She cringed like I'd delivered a knockout punch.
"You called me names, you doubt my credentials.
My fur, this red coat represents all my essentials.
Do I look wild? Like I need a trainer or a mahout?
Okay, for want of a name you may call me Bigfoot."

83

"Wild? I'd say you look particularly petrifying,"
I told her at the risk of horribly dying.
Profusely hairy from head to big foot,
Her colour was tawny with patches of soot.
Brawny arms hung low down to her knees,
Her legs looked like lumber made of some trees.
But strangely, without conveying threat or intimidation,
She was a picture of uncountable contradictions.

84

She sat on a rock on the other side of the pool,
As composedly as one would on a piano stool.
Her head was peaked, her brow very low
From a constant frown that couldn't sulk any more.
Her voice resonated alternatively in bass and baritones,
Like Amrish Puri, like James Earl Jones.
Though terrifying in nature she seemed at tether's end,
Like a penitent antisocial wishing for one good friend.

85

I finally smiled at the threat I had subsided.
This dream could have ended up absolutely one-sided.
Until Ms. Bigfoot chose to rise up once again,
Towering high as if to reaffirm her domain.
But did she sagaciously step back to put me at ease?
She looked disoriented as she shed her hair like fleece!
I stood edgily and held the cudgel up with flair
She abruptly said, "Go on now, let's retire to our lairs."

86

At the blink of an eye she had bound into the vegetation,
Though cudgel in hand I vaulted in the opposite direction;
Headed for our campsite with a story of such absurdity,
Sneha could never include in her notes on biodiversity.
Would the world believe an encounter of this kind?
The Times of India already thinks we're out of our mind!
A Yeti we could report, but not this erudite narcissist.
Sneha's pet page 3 would brand us "cuckoo" or "alarmists."

87

With such brooding thoughts I arrived at the camp,
Pondering if the defense of the place needed revamp.
More rocks for missiles, some catapults here and there,
A fire-wall perhaps that could singe her precious hair!
What could she want of us even if she raided our place?
In Beyul who needed anything, down even to a shoelace?
Sneha heard my story of the encounter with the Yeti,
She admitted I sounded "original" but smacked incredulity!

88

I could not sleep too well in the night,
Expecting Ms.Bigfoot to suddenly visit our campsite.
Though in the dark I heard no barking from Yelp,
And over the next day, as I reasoned with myself.
Is it probable that I could have hallucinated such a wonder?
That a Yeti named Bigfoot and I had an urbane encounter!
And were we the only four creatures on this soil?
Sneha, myself, Yelp and this bristly red gargoyle?

89

Sneha listened to my story, smiling and wide eyed,
With exaggerated gestures her head shook side to side.
I narrated all that had occurred till she finally burst into a laugh,
"I might have reasons to believe your extraordinary story by half
If you had bothered to take our camera instead of a spike."
"Snaps, she is shy," I said. "Photograph her and she may strike!"
"I have my academics," Sneha reminded me. "I keep myself busy.
"If your imagination is fired, it will have to wait dear Mr.
Disney!"

90

She dismissed the whole story like it was some childish lie,
That I'd perhaps made up to entertain her for being her guy.
Another of Beyul's fringe rewards? You never upset your date!
A girlfriend who didn't wonder where you've been so late!
Someday I'll have to convince her of my strange rendezvous.
This creature was a monster! Not Disney's Winnie-the-Pooh
Humiliating, frustrating, but in some insanely surreptitious way
My "madness" liberated me. Big Foot became routine getaway!

91

It was a week before my courage was fully repaired,
But armed with a sling-shot I'd carefully prepared,
I returned to the forest all equipped to fight a riot.
If it worked for David, why not against Mrs. Goliath?
I had to know what this creature was really all about,
Solving the riddle of the Yeti was now paramount.
It isn't every day that you hear of monkeys speak.
I had to at least confirm that I had run into a freak!

92

So back in the woods, more stealthily this time,
I ventured past the white fields of flowering thyme.
Through the living museum of the finest furniture wood,
Until I arrived where a week before I'd resolutely stood.
A rock placed in my vulcanized natural rubber slingshot
Was stretched ready to land on the monster's soft spot.
To my surprise she was there on her piano-stool rock,
Laughing like a large Buddha I'd seen reclining in Bangkok.

93

Basking in the sunlight on the other side of the pool,
You could see she knew she was the queen of Beyul.
My earlier remarks must have had some effect on her brain,
For she was washing herself thoroughly over and over again.
She dipped into the pool several times, often on her knees.
I could smell crushed aromatic herbs blowing in the breeze.
Armed though I was, I still resolved to keep her in conversation,
So I gave a friendly wave, she waved back without hesitation.

94

"Hello Jo, you nitwit, what weapons have you today?
There are no creatures here but us and a little stray."
"Oh, you mean Yelp!" I countered, finding dialogue comforting.
"If you're really his mistress here, well, that's something!"
"That's a long story, Jo! There's plenty of time for that.
Yelp, as you call him, is the only company I've had.
Now I see you're keeping some peace and decorum,
Do you by chance have some hair lotion or serum?"

95

I shook my head and tried to look less threatening,
But this hair-thing of hers was a little disquieting.
"Can I ask you some questions, Ms. Bigfoot Ma'am?
How of all the languages on earth did English you fathom?"
She ignored my queries and stared steadfast into the pool
I didn't repeat myself for fear of breaking some local rule.
Her silence was deafening, it made me ill at ease,
Till she came up with, "Hey Jo, is mine hair or fleece?"

96

Now it dawned on me that this strange obsession,
Which could have been due to some brain concussion,
Had best be left ignored. I must not act too plucky;
For having met a coherent monkey, I should be lucky!
To keep her in conversation I stupidly said, "You're, eh…big!"
"It's my hair I'm talking about. About my breasts I care a fig."
I don't blame her for assuming what I was talking about,
She was waist deep in water and they were all that stood out.

97

"Where did you pick up Yelp?" The Chihuahua dog I meant.
She shrugged and said, "I know that loafer now lives in
your tent.
I've known him long enough. His bark is no symphony!
I didn't find him. The stray followed me around for company."
She was back on her rock, having washed herself enough,
Patting down long tresses so it didn't show she was in the buff.
And as she dried, fluffed, expanded in size, her long hair aflutter,
Back came her crazy quips. "Now doesn't my hair smell better?"

98

For once she clearly smiled, a hideous kind nevertheless
And raised her hands like Mother Mary as if she wanted to bless.
"Jo, how long shall we stand on two sides of a pool
When there are many more places to show you in Beyul?"
She sounded sincere and harmless, understanding my fear.
I asked, "Could I trust you for the rest of our days here?"
"Come, wade across," she said. "I don't wish to wet my coat.
Or swim, you won't find the water even up to your throat."

99

Into the pool I took the plunge and to the hand that was offered.
I thought of Neil Armstrong and the famous lines he'd uttered!
Were we, man and missing-link, creating this moment of history?
Was this going to be the end of a long and confused mystery?
As I came ashore she stepped aside in a courteous kind of way.
This moment had to be historic. This could be an annual day!
"I like plaits but it tugs at my skin. I feel like I'm being bitten!"
I sighed. Resigned to admitting such history needn't be written.

100

But she kept her word and I suffered no hurt or harm;
Her size was a misnomer; her attitude was civil and warm.
A light-footed, gentle giant; child-like in many a way,
Ugly to behold, but this time I wasn't running away.
With some inexplicable shyness at having me so close,
She began walking away with a smile I couldn't diagnose.
Remembering to ignore her occasional hair-related issues,
I followed, wondering why her coat raised queries and rues.

101

Anyway, there I was at Beyul, walking side by side
With a half-ton erect bi-ped as my local guide.
And for many such days we'd meet by her bathing pool,
Returning by dusk having roamed many parts of Beyul.
I wondered if her genus was the Gigantopithecus ape,
Her gait was exactly like the Youtube Patterson tape.
If she was the Yeti or an ape of Darwin's missing link,
Her general knowledge and lexis made you want to rethink.

102

We spoke a lot in the first phase of our exploratory walks,
Days we spent just probing each other only through our talks.
She was fairly up-to-date with goings-on outside Beyul,
But when you tried to find out how, she was stubborn like a mule.
I tried many times to analyze the source of her information,
This place didn't have radio, newspaper or television.
Yet she could just talk about anything under the sun!
Even if it wasn't important she would bring it up for fun.

103

The day came when I confidently marched Sneha to the pool,
Her curiosity had reached a pitch of impatience and ridicule.
"Where on earth did you meet a Yeti that said things to you?
Such things only happen in movies, even such movies are few.
Beyul may be diverse biologically, but it isn't Alice's wonderland;
If some monkey is speaking a language, I'd like to see it firsthand.
Dwelling long in isolation, imagination at times does an upswing.
Jo, are you leaving camp each day to smoke weed or something?"

104

So I marched her to the pool holding her firmly by my side,
Her smug demeanor indicated she still believed I had lied.
She even wore a half-smile; did I see a tongue in her cheek?
She had this ability to deride you without the need to speak!
So, when we arrived at the pool, my chest proudly in a swell,
Sneha serenely looked around her and calmly asked, "Well?"
On the other side of the water stood Ms Bigfoot's rocky stool,
But Bigfoot was not to be seen anywhere near her bathing pool.

105

"Hey, Ms. Bigfoot!" I yelled, searching for marks of her big feet.
"Here, meet my girl," I cried, deliberately sitting on her seat.
"Hang on, she'll emerge! She's late, but she must be on her way;
She's a shy type, but you'll definitely meet my creature today."
We waited in silence. Sneha muffled a giggle at least thrice;
I waited patiently knowing a glimpse of the beast was suffice
To transform Sneha's complacency, have her crying out for help!
Remember her panic when she first met the Chihuahua, Yelp?

106

I couldn't understand the reason, but Ms. Bigfoot didn't show up,
I wouldn't have objected even if she didn't quite meet us close-up.
I searched and could not find a footprint, even a trace of hair,
I realized I could not look for her for I neither knew her lair.
Sneha now looked worried. "Jo, have you had a concussion?
I was playing along for the fun. I realize now it's an obsession!
Come to your senses, sweetheart! It was all your imagination,
You really are now a victim of our long exile and privation."

107

"Bigfoot! Bigfoot! Why did she not keep our appointment?"
Sneha looked even more worried at my disappointment.
"Oh Jo, poor Jo", she sobbed softly, looking at me with pity.
"Snaps! I swear I've been roaming with a very tame Yeti."
"Of course, you've been Jo. Can we now return to camp?
You need rest, Jo. Lately you've been looking like a tramp."
I agreed feebly. That monkey had made me look like a freak.
I was so angry at Ms Bigfoot I decided to forsake her for a week.

108

And so it transpired that from that day I mostly stayed at home,
Even when the Chihuahua taunted me out I just refused to roam.
Day after day I lazed, reading up Sneha's notes on my hammock,
Often wondering what that monkey was doing alone on her rock.
Sneha never referred again to that disappointing episode,
I think she became convinced that I had somehow "cured."
Well, destiny has its ways, and in the week that ensued
Both our lives took a turn in a way we never presumed.

109

Now dear reader, this is where our story does a flip-flop,
Altered circumstances have caused my narration to stop.
Disinclined though I am to swap this recitation with Sneha,
I think she too needs to recount her part of our odd saga.
So with due apologies I hand this chronicle over to my girl
I may not agree with her version or all that she'll unfurl
But our adventures at Beyul with a jabbering Yeti to boot
Would not be complete without her version of "Bigfoot."

PART – 2

110

Sneha is my name but he prefers to call me Snaps.
I need to butt in here before the story he recaps
Is embellished with inaccuracies and routine male prejudice.
Above all, my version has the parts that really went amiss
In his account of our story. My dear reader, sit back.
Sneha is doing the telling now and it's right on track.
Had I narrated this story first and spared this repetition
It would not have needed editing and all this correction.

111

Jo really believes Ashish and Rahul are obstacles.
Boyfriends of mine whose names raises Jo's hackles.
He could be a pit-bull when you mention their names;
I've heard his teeth grind when I treat them like old flames.
I admire Jo's strength and wallow in his jealousy,
But at planning a holiday he was right down lousy.
Beyul was a secret place I visited every two years,
An undisclosed destination whenever the snow clears.

112

It wouldn't be right to believe Jo. Even if he was clever,
He could stupidly drag a joke seemingly forever.
Now to recount this trek, let's go back to the clincher,
I need to take you back near the beginning of our adventure.
Dear reader, something's muddled in Jo's narration of this,
You wouldn't blame him if you knew *why* he went amiss.
Let's go back to the craggy knoll outside the mountain's rear
The day the Sherpas "abandoned" us, seemingly out of fear.

113

Sherpas are old friends of mine; did you even have an inkling?
They were only gathered there to start our regular gamboling.
The trek was my idea. Jo only succumbed to the power of suggestion.
I subconsciously had him believe that finding Beyul was my obsession.
So I had my Sherpa Jamling arrange the jeep for us,
And Sherpas Dawa and Dorgie to head near the mountain pass.
Gombu prepared the secret potion which Jo mistook for wine!
Boy, did we have a hearty laugh when he labeled it "divine"!

114

A note here about Sherpa Gombu will not be out of place:
His father was a Sherpa, his mother was of the same race.
Gombu was a student of Tibetan medicine and Kalachakra,
But his spirit of experimentation made his scruples like lycra!
One summers day in Lhasa he discovered an ancient text
Of secret tonics and elixirs which he decided to put to test.
It caused an unsuspecting lama to develop female breasts,
Evicting Gombu from monastic life and Buddha's other quests.

115

Gombu, Dawa and Dorgie packed our stuff on a mule,
With Jamling and myself leading the way to Beyul.
Jo reeled as he walked the snow, the "wine" working on him;
His silly grin was obvious though his perception was dim.
The details were discussed; we were ready for the climbing.
I bade farewell to Sherpa Dorgie, to Dawa and to Jamling.
Only Gombu trailed us warily, to see his miracle working
The potion was indeed potent. Jo was slowly transforming.

116

A whole day of climbing until dusk hour,
Brought us to a gorge we could barely maneuver.
Jo grew bigger though his clothes looked tragic
The potion he had drunk began working its magic
I was glad all the while as we were descending,
That the route to Beyul was nearing its ending.
Having marched before on that winding rocky maze,
I knew it would take a day more to our mountain face.

117

A storm was upon us as we reached the secret gap,
The passageway to my Beyul. (Not seen on any map!)
As expected, Jo began to tear off his clothes,
Oblivious of the cold, nor worried that he froze.
On his body and limbs, he had sprouted shaggy hair;
He was three feet taller and his face a scary affair,
As we halted at the fissure, the gap in the rocks
Which divided the mountain into two massive blocks.

118

Now, is such a thing possible, you may wish to debate.
An elixir that transforms a man into a giant primate!
Very little is known of Tibetan medicine in our world.
What happens in that mountain kingdom is often unheard.
I did have fears of what could happen if left with an ape alone.
What if he has a sudden surge of wicked testosterone?
Or if the magic potion caused him to fail to recognize me!
Would he behave like how King Kong did with Naomi?

119

I kept up conversation as instructed by Sherpa Gombu
To keep Jo conscious as he fleshed out and grew.
It would take a few hours more for our secret potion
To take full hold of all his senses and motion.
I insisted we hoist a flag at the entrance
And adamantly demanded for his assistance
To put up a sign that said we had first shown,
The only mountain-pass to this region unknown.

120

You see that's the first part Jo couldn't recall
He doesn't remember growing ten feet tall
Under the influence of that potion - so divine!
That Gombu blended with the Nepalese wine.
Anyway, Gombu stopped trailing us at this point;
His job was done; the wine didn't disappoint.
As planned, I was now left with an able bodyguard.
My pit-bull had grown into a fine Saint Bernard!

121

Of our trek to Beyul now all that remained
Was a cleft through which my secret valley drained.
The pass, our passage, this gap in the wall face
Led up to Beyul, a mysterious enclosed space.
The entrance was scary to attempt in the night.
We would have to wait until dawn and some daylight.
Besides, Gombu's potion in Jo's system now slowed.
I knew that from how he slumped, the way he dozed.

122

So I looked for opportunities to feed Jo a fresh dose,
Spiking his morning coffee minutes before he arose.
The potion worked instantly with an energy overflow
He growled as he stretched and was up, rearing to go.
The creature he now was gave his strides needed length,
For from this point on he would need greater strength
To ensure that his steps didn't miss, slip or falter
And he becomes a gentle, caring and obedient porter.

123

We navigated the pass and leapt over large boulders,
Jo gingerly carrying me on his now broad shoulders.
You see, it takes a creature of that strength and size
To traverse this mountain chasm over melting ice.
My voice was his command; he obeyed like a trained pet,
He waded through water without getting me wet.
What might have taken a human trekker eternity
I was accomplishing now with a little impunity.

124

He moved with King Kong strides, lopes and leaps,
I could hear twitters, chirps, clicks and even shrieks
Of cicada, fly, beetle and creatures far and near,
Larger animals if any were perhaps frozen in fear.
Two hours on his shoulder finally slowed Jo's locomotion;
It was again time to dose him with Gombu's magic potion.
Besides he was often stopping, gazing at his reflection
Something I couldn't allow to happen in this expedition.

125

"There's no danger, Jo; no flippant Yeti's at large."
I thought that reassured and showed him who was in charge!
"We'll reach the Beyul valley soon; Jo, you're tired to the bone."
Let's rest awhile. Our trek to the valley we'll postpone."
He grunted and slumped on a rock, his hairy frame to relax,
Drinking water, I mixed in Gombu's magic potion flask.
"The sooner we reach Beyul" he growled, "the sooner we get out.
Snowfall here is sudden, and completely shuts the mouth."

126

The creature was concerned, his human side showing
Despite his bizarre transformation and his red eyes glowing.
He could still communicate in a bass and baritone voice,
Think human thoughts when needed, but limited in choice.
I marveled at Gombu's potion, I've seen it work before
It insulated the creature from the cold, frost and snow.
It also made them obedient and passive to some degree.
It suited my every expedition and gave me service for free.

127

Open for only three weeks, before the snowfall triggered,
It was from old legends, folklore and stories that I had figured
That Beyul existed. Despite the belief that it was a myth.
Jo believed this was my first trek here; in fact, this was my fifth.
The first two trips were disastrous; we lost a friend or two
Till the discovery of the potion's recipe and trials by Gombu.
It was an ancient recipe, the Dalai Lama will vouch for that,
It could create a mighty rhinoceros out of a mountain rat.

128

The sudden midday sunlight alarmed my poor Jo,
He once dropped me hard on the rocky path below
The sun passing overhead shone straight into the crevice,
The light really startled him, he panicked at least twice
First when rays hit the ground exposing a small meadow
And again when darkness fell, the sun entering the shadow.
He looked disoriented and found the path deceitful,
Often slipping and slowing my unique ride to Beyul.

129

Jo labored on in fits and starts for two hours in the pass,
By evening we had neared an open field of familiar grass.
Finally reaching Beyul, I leapt off the creature's shoulder,
Taking breaths of fresh air that was certainly less colder.
If all went well we would camp in Beyul for three weeks,
There was nobody else here to see that we were really two freaks.
I commanded Jo to start the arduous task of camping.
It was a marvel to see how the creature was adapting.

130

Like some scene out of The Planet of the Apes,
Jo fashioned two clubs of varying shapes.
Demonstrating to me attacks he'd planned
Upon intruders whether single or in a band.
I sincerely hoped the wild primate in him
Wasn't as violent and scheming as in the film.
But at constructing a camp of sticks and stones
His animal instincts were certainly well honed.

131

I think it was about now that I first heard Yelp was alive!
A bark in the distance to indicate he had heard us arrive
He was a dog that had accompanied my first expedition
A decade ago! Shouldn't he have died of malnutrition?
God all mighty! Could this Chihuahua really be alive?
Or was it the dog's ghost that somehow managed to survive?
It was cause for alarm. The first time I showed fear.
Jo sensing my uneasiness gave the sound more ear.

132

Only when the barking subsided I felt more at ease,
I passed out in exhaustion, into a slumber of peace.
But not before speculating about this ghost over again;
Could Yelp have survived so long in this mysterious glen?
For why had I not found him in my last four Beyul trips?
And where in Beyul could he have learnt his survival tips?
I had counted every creature here to the last fungi and spore
And my study of biodiversity told me there were no more.

133

Jo was startled in the morning by the first rays of light
For this creature it must be such an otherworldly sight.
Thick forests, mist, grasslands, hot-springs and a geyser.
Though witnessing all of which he seemed none the wiser.
I wondered what went through his giant primate mind;
It must look like paradise for a creature of his kind.
His shaggy coat fluffed in the sun where he sat to bask,
I mixed one more dose of potion for him in Gombu's flask.

134

I kept him distracted. The potion he had to partake.
"We're in a volcano's caldera, Jo!" I talked. "Once a lake.
The rocky sides wore down and soil filled this great bowl."
As long as Jo kept ingesting it I knew I was in control.
"Drink up!" I said and continued, "There was a crack,
On the South side of this valley from eons way back."
He drank the water I had offered, to keep him in form
It made him once again ready to obey and conform.

135

Like a Neanderthal, whenever we roamed around Beyul
Jo tried to gather firewood, twigs and such items for fuel.
I wondered if he had spied me biting into my hamburger,
If Gombu was right the creature should not feel any hunger.
He once growled, "When had we last eaten, Snaps?
Did I eat something which I can't recall perhaps?"
But apart from that inquiry, his hunger and appetite was gone.
My purpose was served. Gombu's potion as usual had won.

136

Dear reader, you may now ignore Jo's sworn testament.
It was he and not I who was the chronic abstinent.
It was his taste buds that made edibles taste like fodder.
He found foodstuff distasteful and repelled by its odour.
I didn't have to cook, I had stocked food in cans and tins
From my previous trips to Beyul along with multi vitamins.
Oblivion of hunger was common, loathing for food quicker
With people who've had a brush with Gombu's elixir.

137

I could not risk subjecting Jo to any dehydration,
Occasionally he drank water which I timely mixed with potion.
I often wondered if he remembered Rahul or even Ashish,
Now that he was smote with something stronger than hashish.
He needed water often, he thirsted more than a Bedouin.
It made it convenient for me to give him Gombu's medicine.
To feed him the potion on time I would have to take great pain;
A seven-hour lapse could transform him back into little Jo
again

138

On our first day in Beyul Jo secured the camp
And I kept a flame kindled in a small hurricane lamp,
We set a hearth of stones and kept another fire
For coffee and hot food in case I was to tire.
Jo explored our neighborhood along the stream
Treading the sand bank bare-feet as if in a dream.
I joined him in these excursions out of curiosity
To complete my notes on Beyul's biodiversity.

139

This became routine for many days in the valley,
When I didn't feel like walking Jo would carry.
Over great distances, streams, grasslands and slopes,
While I took pictures, made sketches and notes.
He was eager to enter Beyul's great foreboding forest.
I forbade him. The primate might be put to the test.
Gombu had warned that I could lose control of him
Trees were his habitat. He could disappear in a whim.

140

For over a week we roamed over familiar terrain
Mostly on his shoulder. I felt like Tarzan's Jane.
Having compiled enough material to do my thesis
With photographs and samples to form a basis
For an awesome submission that'll top the university
Earning me a gold medal on the subject of biodiversity.
But time was also running out. I just had to really hurry
In case untimely snowfall filled the mountain-pass in a flurry.

141

So, in another day or two I repacked my haversack,
Not much of Gombu's potion remained in the flask.
Perhaps just enough to fuel our return trip back home,
To ride the difficult zones astride this monkey's clone.
As always I left the campsite undisturbed and intact,
For use in a future expedition should I need to reenact.
I posted a few notices, reminders, items to inventorize,
Then sparingly poured Jo's potion for him to revitalize.

142

Ere we got started we heard the eerie yelping sound again,
Carried in the wind, like a ghostly cry of panic and pain.
Downwind from miles away, was it a cry for help?
The abandoned Chihuahua! It surely cannot be Yelp!
Sounds over great distances are hard to measure here
But I couldn't help but feel a sense of alarm and fear.
Each bark was louder like the dog was approaching us.
How quickly could we depart before it caught us up?

143

Jo grew extremely protective, holding his wooden cudgel,
He picked me up on his shoulder like a guardian angel.
We set off at a brisk pace, ears strained to hear the bark,
Striding hard to reach the passage before it became dark.
As much as I feared the ghost of this Chihuahua dog,
I dreaded the bashing it would get with Jo's wooden log.
I couldn't help but sniffle out loud in utter fear and woe,
If Yelp was really alive I didn't want him killed by Jo.

144

Jo appeared to believe it was a rabid wolf or fox,
Hot on our trail sniffing my haversack or food stock.
We ran, stumbled and staggered only in time to find
Our passage was filling up. Ice and snow combined
With slush and rocks from the cliffs fell into the pass.
We were sealed in. The landslide blocked every chance.
I recalled Gombu's warning, my hands upon my brow,
Of the possibility, however rare, of untimely snow.

145

The persistent yelping now made us both spin around.
Jo picked up his cudgel, swung it and hit the ground.
"Please," I cried, "It might just be a harmless rat or frog!"
Though I knew such loud barking could only be a dog.
I stood there fear-stricken! Jo could never quite realize
That it was once a pet of ours he was about to pulverize!
Neither could I now begin to tell him about an old dog
That we had lost many years ago on an evening walk.

146

The creature came around the bend wagging a little tail,
I froze seeking a mark of a ghost. Some sign? Some tell-tale?
We must have looked comic, the primate and I in our fear,
Of a Chihuahua in front of us with a mountain in the rear.
God all mighty, it was Yelp! Lost dog of our old expedition!
As healthy as I had known him then. No signs of deprivation!
He sat there valiantly, wagging a noodle for a tail,
Was this what I'd feared this time so often in this dale?

147

Jo relaxed when he comprehended it was a pathetic dog
"Hey Snaps! That doesn't look like a venomous frog!
But what's a dog doing alone in Beyul?" growled Jo
"He looks less like a dog, more like a spot on the floor."
From ten feet high Jo could barely see the dog below;
I'm sure he could have crushed it with just his big toe.
"He's doesn't appear to be wild," I said. "He needs help.
He's a small breed. A Chihuahua. Let's call him Yelp."

148

Jo stared in confusion as the dog snuggled up to me,
Bobbing up and down in joy, his tail wagging in glee.
Familiar behavior betrayed that he knew me from before,
But fortunately it didn't make Jo suspicious or sore.
Instead he played with the dog like it was his pet too,
And tried to feed him biscuits which he refused to chew.
But as the passage clogged with snow I felt all alone,
Despite the Chihuahua and my transmutated Yeti clone.

149

Prospects of being trapped for a year was now a reality.
And if my stock of food ran out I was inviting a calamity.
I wasn't sure if Yelp needed feeding or how he survived,
I wondered on what food he lived but he had surely thrived.
There was some more potion in Gombu's flask for Jo,
To transmutate for a week. But I would need some more.
As we retraced our steps back to the camp of our creation,
I knew I should not panic. I had to work out our salvation.

150

I felt fear and a weariness, like I'd never felt before.
"I should never have attempted this," I loudly swore.
Feeling weak in the knees I sat down to ease my shock,
Jo unhitched my haversack and squatted on a rock.
I had always entered Beyul and exited with ease;
It was too early in the year for the passage to freeze!
Or were we wrong? Was it just the mouth of the pass
That experienced a minor landslide causing the impasse?

151

In which case there was a chance, some hope,
By tackling the fallen sludge to make our way home.
If only I could climb over the debris to unravel,
If the passage beyond was clear enough to travel.
Cutting a path through the rubble would be very slow,
We needed to somehow climb over the ice and snow.
And peek into the mountain pass, the passage beyond.
Jo could do that, but what if he chose to abscond?

152

I could not risk that. My only passport to freedom,
As long he was within Beyul I could contain him.
In the days that followed our failed attempt to exit,
Jo showed restlessness. The woods he wished to visit
Beckoned him. I thought it best to let the creature roam,
Despite Gombu's advice, this was vacation home.
It also gave me some privacy to try a little experiment,
To peek over the landslide and make my own judgment.

153

Next day at dawn Jo strolled into the grassy valley,
I let him go quite assured Beyul was a blind alley.
Heading towards the woods beyond the grassy swamp,
Even if I lost him awhile he'd find his way to camp.
This was my opportunity, this new found isolation,
To plan my escape from this doomed vacation.
I had a plan. A risky one. But hell, I've dared before!
Gombu's magic could work for me if it could work for Jo.

154

By transmutating into a Yeti I could head to the frontier,
Climb the sludge and snow to check if the pass was clear.
I needed just a small dose from Gombu's enchanted flask,
To tide over this emergency. To accomplish this task.
With Jo away and Yelp asleep, I poured myself a peg,
Its divine taste belied the fact that it was a powder keg!
I wasn't aware I grew until my undergarments snapped,
My adrenaline rushed before all my clothes unwrapped!

155

Hair! Boundless hair! That thing of such beauty!
I grew so much of it that I almost felt snooty.
I admired the length and its tawny lush to boot,
If Jo looked like a Yeti, then I must be Bigfoot!
Hair had been so scarce; I'd never had as a human,
Seeing it in such profusion, I finally felt like a woman!
In that devil-may-care mood of sheer exhilaration,
I drank some more from the flask in my elation.

156

I bounded out of camp in the direction of the pass,
Over streams, boulders, shrubs and endless grass.
In a jiffy I had reached the cleft in the rock face,
Where sludge, ice and snow had worked to deface,
Our passage out of Beyul blocked by the landslide.
I climbed over the rubble to see what it had to hide.
Lo and behold! As I stood on the top of the fallen pile,
The passage behind was fine! All clear for a mile!

157

Since the snow hadn't begun any untimely fall,
We could still make it if we both climbed this wall
Of sludge and ice. Except the dog who would need help.
This time I was determined not to leave behind Yelp.
But to achieve this feat we both had to remain "Yeti".
To Jo I would have to reveal my secret. What a pity?
Gombu's secret had remained my undisclosed concoction,
Till this turn of events now forced its revelation.

158

But first I had to find Jo wherever he had gone to loiter,
Somewhere in the woods I would have to reconnoiter.
So while the adrenaline still soared in my hot veins,
I bounded past our camp and into the grassy plains,
Searching for Jo, wondering how to lure him back.
When he sees me thus transformed would he attack?
Dear reader, it was awkward when I found him though.
I was now the creature! The Yeti had shrunk back to "Jo."

159

The magic potion in Jo had worn out its efficacy,
He was downsized to human, with not a hint of Yeti.
We both expressed shock, fear and incredulity,
He, startled by my form and me by his nudity!
Jeez! He hadn't even recognized who I was!
Standing shamelessly. Was he expecting applause?
But I could also sense his fear and reckless bravado.
Embarrassed, I proceeded to drink water with gusto.

160

But when he wiggled his nose I felt that was sassy,
If I smelt a little putrid, he wasn't exactly spicy.
But he twitched his nostrils and gagged in excess,
Was he frightened, teasing or simply in stress?
There was a moment when I thought he would run.
I would have enjoyed just chasing him for fun!
Should I try talking? Engage him in conversation,
Before giving him the story of my transformation?

161

I cleared my throat, the sound made me laugh,
I wondered if I could articulate like Jo by half.
Thinking sign-language might put him at ease,
I saluted him to indicate I had come in peace.
It made matters worse, he was poised to strike,
With a flimsy twig which ended in a spike.
"Do you like my coat?" I somehow articulated.
He looked all around as if I had ventrilocated!

162

It was time to give him a piece of my mind.
Talking calmly to which he seemed disinclined.
"Boy! In your aggression I don't see any threat.
You look even weaker when you sweat.
Look at you, you scrawny little soul,
Take it easy. Exercise some self- control!"
Then it occurred to me; if he chooses to be hostile,
Why not toy with him just for a little while?

163

Now opportunity favoured me and so I dared,
I ruffled, preened then shook and declared,
"Well, what do you think of my furry coat?
Is it better in hue than Gita's Pashmina goat?
I know your world well, I once lived there,
I've seen and experienced your vanity fair.
Now tell me quick just what you think
Of my tawny coat. Is it better than mink?"

164

Jo looked dazed at my verbal barrage,
I think he still believed I was a mirage.
"Okay Yeti girl, just what's it you want?"
He stood up straight to loudly taunt.
Seeing his discomfiture, I laughed aloud,
Heaving my chest to show how I was proud,
To remind him of his silly old Gita Singh!
"Does my coat look like some artificial thing?"

165

And so it went on and on between Jo and me,
Not for a moment did he guess I was *his* Yeti!
He tried talking to me not knowing what was afoot,
He even believed me when I called myself Ms.Bigfoot.
But even as I spoke to him I could feel the magic waning,
Gombu's potion was vanishing, I was transforming.
Shedding hair! "Sneha" he would definitely recognize!
Had I stayed a minute longer to metamorphosize!

166

I abruptly shooed him away so I could quickly decamp,
Making it in leaps and bounds back to our camp.
Arriving naked and sweating, in time to freshen up.
The running had helped; Jo would arrive ere I sup.
With a long fairytale smacking of such absurdity,
I could never include in my notes on biodiversity.
Dear reader, to you this secret I had to disclose
It was the only way out before the pass froze!

167

For a few more days at Beyul I had time to decide,
About being a Yeti myself and trekking by his side.
It was the only way both could now negotiate the pass,
Where snow, slush, ice and rocks had piled up en masse.
The only way out. This time I couldn't make him my porter,
For both of us were required to climb until the last quarter.
If the last drops of Gombu's potion were now to run stale,
It would spell our incarceration for 365 days in this jail.

168

I had had enough of Beyul. This was my last trip there.
I had enough on biodiversity to make my research guide stare.
I had rescued Yelp, there was no reason to return,
I was thankful to the Sherpas, and Gombu's good turn.
The truth was not going to be pleasant for poor Jo,
I had used him as my porter as many others before.
We knew we were in love but I felt some apprehension,
Gita Singh was still out there to offer competition.

169

I'm close to the end of my own narration, dear Reader,
You may not believe my story or Jo's version either.
We made it out, but couldn't make it back to the cities,
We roamed the snowline for days as long as we were Yetis.
Local people reported large foot-prints frozen in the snow.
A mountaineer even filmed us for a National Geographic show.
So, that's how I made my last trek to the valley of Beyul,
Did I mention that my earlier porters were Ashish and
Rahul?

Afterword

In conclusion, there's always a lesson learnt,
Some big feet frozen and fingers burnt
In the tumult of relationships in one's life.
I once chased a shadow that was someone's wife.
Purpose and need clash with destiny and fate,
Exposing one's real motive and mental state.
I hope dear Reader that you enjoyed this tale,
If this novella stirred you, do send me a mail.

About the Author

 Born in Cannanore, Kerala, Jo Nambiar was an athlete, an equestrian and also holds a Master's Degree in Kung Fu. In the 1980s as a Physical Educationist at the International Youth Centre, New Delhi, his students of unarmed combat included members of the Delhi Police, Indo-Tibetan Border Police, the Assam Rifles and the President's Body Guard. He worked as a Tea Planter with The Assam Company for over a decade. He has acted in Shakespearean as well as contemporary theatre. As a numismatist, Nambiar has one of the largest collections of ancient coins and rare currencies in the country which has global recognition. Nambiar has the distinction of being the Convener of the largest Children's Carnival in the world, the "BALA MELA" for underprivileged children every year at Bangalore. He is also a painter and a sculptor.